ORCHARD BOOKS
96 Leonard Street, London EC2A 4RH
Orchard Books Australia
14 Mars Road, Lane Cove, NSW 2066
First published in Great Britain 1993
First paperback publication 1993
Text © Rose Impey 1993
Illustrations © Shoo Rayner 1993
The right of Rose Impey to be identified as the author
and Shoo Rayner as the illustrator of this work has
been asserted by them in accordance with the
Copyright, Designs and Patents Act, 1988.
A CIP catalogue record for this book
is available from the British Library.
Hardback 1 85213 451 8
Paperback 1 85213 452 6
Printed in Great Britain

(*Tenrecs are small shrew-like creatures which
live in caves in Madagascar. They have very
large litters.)

TOO MANY BABIES

Mrs Tailless was a tenrec.*
She was worn out.
She was like the old woman
who lived in a shoe
(except *she* lived in a cave).
Mrs Tailless had so many children
she didn't know what to do.
Mrs Tailless had *thirty-one* babies!

Thirty-one mouths to feed.
Thirty-one faces to wash.

Thirty-one babies
to tuck in each night.
And Mrs Tailless had to do it
all on her own.

There was Mr Tailless, of course.
But Mr Tailless didn't know
about babies.
Mr Tailless was a teacher.
He knew all about children.
He had thirty-one
in his class at school.
But he didn't know
about babies.

Mr Tailless told his wife
she should teach the babies
to read,

to count to ten,

to tell the time,

to write their names.

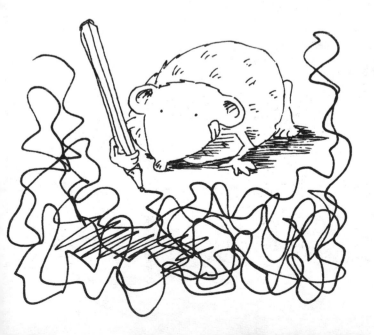

But poor Mrs Tailless
was too busy
to teach them anything.

One day she said to her husband,
"It is hard work, minding babies."
Mr Tailless said,
"Not as hard as teaching,
my dear."

"Perhaps we should
swop for a day," said Mrs Tailless.
"Then we would see which is harder."
"Very well," said her husband.
So that is what they did.

Next morning, very early,
Mrs Tailless went to work.
Mr Tailless stayed in bed.
He was looking forward
to a nice easy day.

Suddenly he heard a noise. Bump!
Then another. Bump!
And another.
Bump! Bump! Bump!

The babies were awake.
They were climbing out of bed
and falling down the stairs
like skittles.

Mr Tailless picked them up
and put them back in bed.
He ran up and downstairs
fifteen times.
He was puffed out.

"Now," said Mr Tailless,
"no one must get out of bed
until I say so."

But the babies kept on
climbing out of their beds
and falling downstairs.
In the end Mr Tailless gave up.

It was well past their
breakfast time.
The babies were hungry.
Mr Tailless put on
a big pan of porridge.

He put the babies in their chairs.
He gave each baby a spoon.
The babies banged their spoons.
The noise was terrible.
"Stop that noise, this minute,"
said Mr Tailless.

But the babies were
having a good time.
They went on banging.
Mr Tailless took the spoons away.
The babies began to cry.
The noise was terrible.

Mr Tailless noticed a smell.
The porridge was burning.
He stirred all the burnt bits in.
Mr Tailless thought the babies
wouldn't notice.
But they did.
The babies took one mouthful
and began to cry.

One or two began to throw
their porridge.
Then all the babies
threw their porridge.
Mr Tailless couldn't believe it.
He took the porridge away.
The babies began to cry *again*.

Now they were covered in porridge.
Mr Tailless had to bath them.
He filled the bath.
He lifted the babies
out of their chairs
and lined them up.
"Now stay there!" he said.

But the babies didn't know about
lining up.
Some of them climbed in the bath.
Some of them climbed
on the furniture.
Some of them rolled on the floor.
There was porridge everywhere.

Mr Tailless put each of the babies
back in its chair.
He was worn out
and it wasn't even break time.

He sat down for a rest.
'Peace at last,' he thought.
But it didn't last.
The babies were bored.
They were crying again.

Mr Tailless thought he would
read them a story.
It was *The Tale of Peter Rabbit*.
He began to read to them.
But the babies didn't know
about rabbits.

They didn't know about beans
and radishes.
They didn't know about stories.
They couldn't even see the pictures.
The babies tried to climb out
of their chairs.
In the end Mr Tailless gave up.

Mr Tailless had been a teacher
for twenty years.
He had never had such
a difficult class.

Mr Tailless decided
to take the babies out.
He put the babies in their pram.
It was a special pram.
It held all thirty-one babies.

Now Mr Tailless felt happy.
'We will go to the park,'
he thought.

'The babies can have some exercise.
It will wear them out.
Perhaps they will sleep later.'

Mr Tailless hoped he would
be able to sleep too.

He pushed the babies in the pram.
It was a long way, downhill.

In the middle of the park
there was plenty of space.
'The babies will be safe
here,' he thought.
He lifted them out.
"Now, everyone must stay
where I can see them," he said.

But the babies disappeared
straightaway.

They found trees to climb.

They found holes to fall down.

They found nasty things to eat.

They found good places to hide.
It took hours to find them all again.

The babies liked the park.
They didn't want to go home.
They began to cry.
The noise was terrible.

It was a long way back.
It was all uphill.
The babies didn't mind.
They slept the whole way.
But Mr Tailless was worn out.

When they got home
the babies woke up.
They had had a lovely sleep.
Now they were hungry.
But Mr Tailless hadn't made
any lunch.
The babies began to cry.
Mr Tailless felt like crying too.

'Babies are very hard work,'
he thought. 'Harder than children.'
Tomorrow he would be glad
to go back to school.

He put the babies in their chairs.
He gave each of them a biscuit.
He sat down in *his* chair
and fell asleep.

Soon Mrs Tailless came home.
She had had a lovely day.
The children were happy
to have a new teacher.
They liked to hear stories
about the thirty-one babies.
And all the tricks they got up to.

But Mrs Tailless had missed
her babies.
She wouldn't want
to leave them *every* day.

"No, one day a week,
would be nice," she said.
"After all, a change
is as good as a rest."
But Mr Tailless was too busy resting
to say anything.

CRACK-A-JOKE

Other great ANIMAL CRACKERS

TINY TIM
The Longest Jumping Frog in the World
Tiny Tim was only a very small frog but he
had a VERY BIG jump. And Tiny Tim had set
his heart on winning the Jumping Jubilee.

HOT DOG HARRIS
The Smallest Dog in the World
Hot Dog was no bigger than a bar of soap or a
bag of chips. So when he set off to explore the
world he had some unexpected adventures.

A BIRTHDAY FOR BLUEBELL
The Oldest Cow in the World
Bluebell was so old – she'd been everywhere
and done everything. Her friends couldn't
decide what to get for a cow who was seventy-
eight years old.